# THE TRANSFORMERS™

AUTOBOTS FIGHT BACK

*written by* JOHN GRANT

*illustrated by* MIKE COLLINS and MARK FARMER

Ladybird Books

Optimus Prime was briefing Bumblebee for a spying mission.

"Find out all you can," he said. "It is most important that we know what the Decepticons' plans are. The safety of the Earth people as well as our own depends on that knowledge."

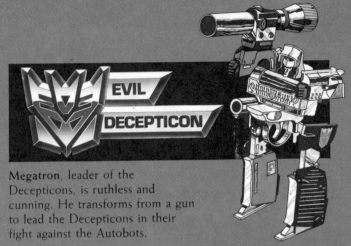

**EVIL DECEPTICON**

**Megatron**, leader of the Decepticons, is ruthless and cunning. He transforms from a gun to lead the Decepticons in their fight against the Autobots.

**Soundwave** transforms from a cassette recorder to a Decepticon communicator robot and acts as a radio link for the other Decepticons. He is able to read minds and will use blackmail for his own gain. Soundwave is despised by all other Decepticons.

**Laserbeak** is cowardly and will run for safety if he is threatened. He can fly at speeds of up to 250 mph and transforms from a spy cassette to the Decepticon interrogation robot.

**Starscream** transforms from a plane to the Decepticon air commander robot. He can fly faster than any of the Decepticons and seeks to replace Megatron as leader. Starscream is ruthless and cruel.

**Rumble** is small and tough. When he transforms from a spy cassette to the demolition robot, he transmits low frequency groundwaves to create powerful earthquakes.

**Ravage** likes to operate alone and is the craftiest of all Decepticons. He transforms from a spy cassette to a saboteur robot. He is very good at hiding himself in the shadows of the night and can walk without making a sound.

Once, long ago, a race of robot beings called Autobots were forced to wage war against another race of robots called Decepticons, to bring peace back to their home planet of Cybertron.

As the war went on, chance brought both sides to Earth. They crashed so violently on landing that all the robots lay in the Earth's crust, seemingly without life, for over four million years.

Suddenly the energy set in motion by a powerful volcanic eruption gives them life once more – and the war starts all over again here on Earth. Among the robots' many strange powers is the ability to transform into other shapes, and they use this to disguise themselves to fit in with the civilisation they find on Earth. The Autobots have to defend themselves, they have to protect this planet with all its valuable resources and the people who live here – and they must also build a new space ship if they are ever to get back to Cybertron...

British Library Cataloguing in Publication Data

Grant, John, 1930-
    The autobots fight back.—(Transformers. Series 853; v. 3)
    I. Title  II. Collins, Mike  III. Farmer, Mark  IV. Series
823'.914[J]    PZ7
    ISBN 0-7214-0942-3

First edition

Published by Ladybird Books Ltd  Loughborough  Leicestershire  UK
Ladybird Books Inc  Lewiston  Maine 04240  USA
© MCMLXXXV HASBRO INDUSTRIES, INC. ALL RIGHTS RESERVED
© Artwork and text LADYBIRD BOOKS LTD MCMLXXXV

A few hours later the small Autobot was in sight of the Decepticons' remote mountain stronghold. He scanned the surroundings with his super vision. There were Decepticon look-outs on several vantage points but Bumblebee's special skills lay in his ability to move stealthily and secretly.

Keeping under cover, he reached the inner part of the rocky complex. He followed a narrow tunnel, and found himself looking down into a cavern where Megatron and the more important Decepticons were having a discussion.

"Work on rebuilding the space cruiser is going well," Megatron was saying, "but it will all be in vain if we cannot complete the power system."

"But it *is* complete," said Starscream. "It only needs assembling!"

"It also needs to be tested," said Megatron. "Report, Soundwave."

"ION-DRIVE POWER SYSTEM REQUIRES TEST AND RUNNING-IN...RESTRICTED SPACE IN DECEPTICON BASE UNSUITABLE ...RECOMMEND EXPLORATION."

"We are wasting time!" shouted Starscream. "Testing! Running-in! Is our technology so bad that we cannot trust our own work? If I had *my* way the ion-drive would be in place and we would be already well on our way home to Cybertron!"

"You do *not* have your way," cried Megatron. "And until then, which is unlikely, you will carry out orders."

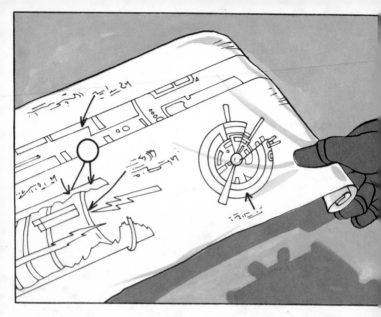

Soundwave produced a roll of plans. Bumblebee craned forward from his hiding place to see, and could just make out the details. It was a design for a giant space-drive test rig which was to be an enormous tube five metres across and sixteen hundred metres long. The inside of the tube would be lined with electronic and electro-magnetic equipment. No wonder the Decepticons were stuck! They had no place to conceal a thing as big as that.

Starscream spoke again. "Why can't the tube be formed by boring into the side of a mountain?"

"We do not have the power for such a huge task," said Megatron.

"We have a great store of energon cubes!" cried Starscream.

"Starscream!" shrieked Megatron. "You try my patience with your stupidity! If we use the energon cubes to dig a tunnel, what would we use for fuel to drive the space cruiser?"

Before Starscream could think of an answer, Soundwave broke in:

"ALARM! ALARM!...INTRUDER DETECTED!...SENSORS INDICATE AUTOBOT!"

Bumblebee fled, with the Decepticons in hot pursuit. He raced back along the narrow tunnel, and scrambled down the rocks as fast as he could go.

On level ground he transformed to his Volkswagen shape and raced off at top speed in a cloud of dust. Shots hit the ground around his wheels as the Decepticons tried to stop him.

"Hold your fire!" cried Megatron. "We are wasting precious energy. Activate Ravage!"

With a snarl the ferocious metal animal leapt off on the trail of the small car.

Ahead the country was hilly and wooded. Bumblebee thought that if he could reach the cover of the woods and hills, he would have a chance of shaking off his pursuer.

Ravage was gaining fast as Bumblebee reached the hills and hit a narrow dirt road which wound through the trees. It took all of the small Autobot's skill to stay on the road as his wheels slipped and skidded on the loose surface. But try as he might, he could not shake off Ravage. Ahead, the dirt road was crossed by a rough track running along the bottom of a deep, narrow gulley. At the exact moment that Ravage loosed one of his missiles, Bumblebee slid in a four-wheel drift off the road and on to the track.

The track was covered with weeds and a layer of dead leaves, and Bumblebee's wheels left easily-followed ruts. Ravage prepared to fire his remaining missile, but Bumblebee was out of sight round a bend in the track. Following the ruts, Ravage bounded round the corner.

Next moment the canine robot crashed into the side of the gulley and tumbled head over heels, blinded by the glare of Bumblebee's headlights in the shade of the high banks. Bumblebee had suddenly remembered that Ravage's weak point was his sensitivity to bright light.

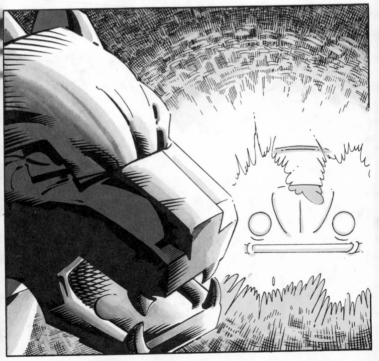

By the time that Ravage had recovered, Bumblebee had made good his escape and was nowhere to be seen. Ravage prowled along the track hoping to pick up the Autobot's trail, but Bumblebee had managed to climb the steep slope leaving no trace on the hard ground.

Growling to himself with rage, Ravage turned a last bend and saw that the gulley came to an abrupt end against a sheer hillside thickly clad in trees and undergrowth. There seemed no way through. Ravage pushed through the bushes and between the trunks of young trees. Soon, he was close to the hillside – and he made a surprising discovery.

There was a wide opening in the hill! Hidden from outside by the trees, a high arched entrance to what must be a cave rose above Ravage's head.

Activating his audio-visual sensors, the Decepticon passed through the arch. It *might* just be the hiding place of the fleeing Autobot spy!

As Ravage made his way carefully into the
darkness of the cave, his sensors recorded much
information. A short distance inside, the
vegetation gave way to a rough stone floor, which
appeared to be level. Two strips of metal ran
down the centre, and there was no exit to be
seen.

Deciding that he had learned enough, Ravage
returned to the open air and made all speed to
report back to Megatron.

Megatron raged about Bumblebee's escape, and

Ravage cowered before his leader. Then he transformed to his cassette shape, and the Decepticons gathered round the play-back monitor.

As the data collected by Ravage's sensors came up on the video-screen, Megatron roared in triumph. "Those miserable Autobots and their clumsy spy have done us a great favour. This cave may be the means of our testing the ion-drive. With luck it will convert easily as a space-drive test rig. I will make a personal inspection."

Led by Ravage, Megatron and Soundwave located the cave. As they explored the interior, Soundwave checked out the dimensions.

"DATA SUGGESTS PRIMITIVE EARTHLING ARTEFACT…PURPOSE UNKNOWN… PARTIAL DESTRUCTION BY ROCKFALL… REMAINING SECTION MEASURES SIXTEEN HUNDRED METRES…DIAMETER FIVE METRES."

"Exactly what we need!" cried Megatron.

"METAL STRIPS SUGGEST CRUDE ENERGY CONDUCTOR SYSTEM."

"Forget those," said Megatron. "Contact base. I want work to start immediately on transporting the equipment. Nothing must stand in the way of assembling the space-drive test rig and testing the ion-drive."

Meanwhile Bumblebee was reporting to Optimus Prime.

"So, it seems the Decepticons are having problems with their ion-drive!" he said.

"More trouble than they're worth," said Trailbreaker. "Give me good old-fashioned neutron-drive every time. This should keep

Megatron and company grounded for a long time to come."

"There's no guarantee of that," said Optimus Prime. "The Decepticons are not only ruthless, they are also highly ingenious. They'll find a way out of their difficulties one way or another... unless, that is, we can do something to stop them. Bumblebee, I want you to return to the Decepticon base and see what else you can find out. And be more careful this time!"

Bumblebee was back with his report by nightfall. The Decepticon base was all but deserted. Megatron and all the more important Decepticons had gone, taking most of the technical equipment with them.

"This is worse than I thought," said Optimus Prime.

Quickly the Autobot leader issued his orders.

"Trailbreaker, take up position on that hill to the south. Keep a listening watch for Decepticon radio signals. They must still keep in touch with their base. And you, Hound, do the same on the ridge due north of here."

Trailbreaker and Hound transformed into their shapes as motor van and jeep and set off in

opposite directions. Once in position, they extended their monitoring aerials and tuned to Decepticon frequency.

The air was alive with Decepticon radio messages. In a very short time both Autobots had recorded all the information they needed, and were hurrying back to base to report to Optimus Prime.

It took only a moment to plot the radio co-ordinates on to a map. Spike, the young human, put his finger on a small range of low hills. "The Decepticons have set themselves up somewhere there," he said.

Spike's father was still studying the map. "This area was once famous for its stone quarries. They're all abandoned now but an abandoned quarry would be just the place for the Decepticons to work undisturbed. It might be worth having a look."

"That will be difficult," said Optimus Prime. "They will be on their guard and will have look-outs posted. This is quite a problem."

"We have another problem," said Spike. "You Autobots don't eat, but humans do. Groceries are getting low. Dad and I could do with going into town to stock up."

"I'll take you," said Ironhide. "I'm built for carrying groceries, and I enjoy a trip into town."

Next morning Ironhide set off with Spike and his father. Spike was behind the wheel. There was a country town some miles from Autobot headquarters. They reached it before mid-day, and parked Ironhide while they went off with their shopping list.

"Hey, you guys," said Ironhide as they packed more goods inside him, "ever think of going on a diet? It would do you good, and it would sure take some of the strain off my suspension."

"We appreciate your effort," said Spike, "and for a treat we're going to get you a can of super-lubricant."

"Gee, thanks!" said Ironhide.

Spike was coming out of the garage shop when a notice caught his eye. It announced a car rally to be held in a few days' time, and showed a map of the course. It passed through the hills along back roads...right through the area where the Decepticons had set up their new base.

This might be just what the Autobots were looking for!

Back at base, Spike explained his idea to Optimus Prime.

"On the day of the rally, the back roads will be busy with cars. The Decepticons can't stop all traffic because it would reveal their presence. I suggest that we take part in the rally."

"Good thinking, Spike," said Optimus Prime. "Jazz can be our entry in the rally, with you as driver. Transformed, I can easily transport an Autobot battle unit, ready to strike when you and Jazz locate the Decepticons."

Spike's father had been studying the map once more. "The route crosses the line of an old railway," he said. "And that line leads to one of the old quarries – the only one big enough to be shown on the map. My guess is that the Decepticons are holed up there."

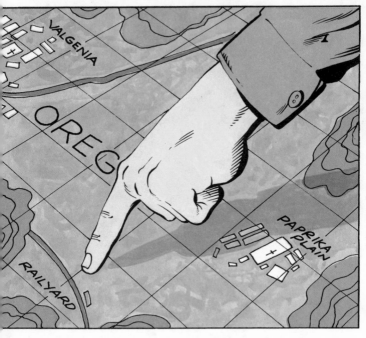

Optimus Prime set about issuing detailed instructions to the Autobots who were to form the battle unit. Ratchet called to Jazz, "Come with me. If you're going rallying, you'll have to be in top condition. I'll give you a complete tune-up."

ANNUAL CAR RALLY

On the day of the rally, the Autobots left their base early. Spike travelled as driver in Jazz, who had transformed into his sports car shape for the occasion. Spike's father was in the cab of Optimus Prime's articulated truck. The rest of the Autobot battle unit were inside the truck.

The town square from which the rally was to start was crowded with people. Flags flew. A band played. And marshals guided the competitors to the start. As a late entry, Spike was one of the last to start.

At last Jazz stood on the starting line, his engine revving. The starter counted down, "FIVE…FOUR…THREE…TWO…ONE…" and dropped the flag. With a roar of exhaust and a screech of tyres, Jazz shot across the line.

Spike pretended to drive until they had left the crowds behind. Then he took out the map again. The old railway and quarry were situated about half-way through the third stage of the rally course.

OREGON

He spoke to Jazz. "If the Decepticons *are* in the old quarry, they will be watching the road near it. I want to look at the quarry on foot. You will

have to drop me off without the Decepticons guessing that you are not a proper rally car."

"It'll be tricky," said Jazz. "Dangerous, too. After I've dropped you, I'll carry on for a bit then come back and join you across country. You need me to communicate with Optimus Prime and the battle unit."

"Quiet, now!" said Spike. "There's a check-point coming up!"

As they cleared the second check-point Spike said, "Any time now!"

The road wound through the hills, with thick woods on either side. Then they were running steeply downhill. Ahead, the road swung left round a blind corner. And round the corner there was the dull glint of rusty metal across the road.

"That's it!" cried Spike. "The old railway! Slow down, Jazz!"

Jazz dropped down to third, then to second gear. Spike had the door open ready, and Jazz braked for a moment. The sports car slowed and Spike threw himself on to the grass verge.

As he rolled over and over, he heard Jazz accelerate up the next hill and into the distance. With any luck a Decepticon look-out would not realise that the car had slowed right down, nor notice that it no longer had a driver.

Spike rose to his feet. He looked carefully around, then began to follow the rusty railway track up to the quarry.

Spike crept stealthily from tree to tree as he followed the track. It was very quiet. There was no hum of machinery. No sound of voices. He kept his eyes open for the shine of metal. But there was nothing.

At the top of the long slope he found the quarry.

It was deserted, both by men *and* Decepticons. Everything was overgrown. There were the ruins of several buildings and a stone-crushing plant. On the rusty rails stood an abandoned train of half a dozen rusty hopper wagons.

At that moment Jazz came back, appearing from among the trees.

"They're not here," said Spike. He took out his map again. "I bet *that's* where they are," he cried excitedly. "We went the wrong way. The railway leads to an old tunnel. Quick, see if you can call up Optimus Prime!"

"Good thinking, Spike," said the Autobot leader when Spike explained about the tunnel. "The Decepticons are bound to have fortified the tunnel mouth, but your dad says that railway tunnels have air shafts. We'll surprise them by dropping in. Stand by for further instructions."

"I'd like to take a look," said Jazz. "Same here," said Spike.

The two made their way cautiously back down to the road and across it. They followed the winding railway cutting...and there was the tunnel. The Decepticons had partly cleared away the undergrowth and the tunnel was brightly lit.

Complex machinery glowed with power as preparations went ahead for the ion-drive test.

Jazz's radio crackled. It was Optimus Prime. "We have located a hidden air shaft. We are about to launch our attack. Stand by to give support."

Nothing happened for a moment, then Soundwave's alarm call echoed from the tunnel: "ALARM! ALARM!...INTRUDERS!... AUTOBOT INTRUDERS!"

At Optimus Prime's command, the Autobots dropped through the air shaft firing their weapons as they went. Caught by surprise, the Decepticons retreated. Then Megatron's voice rang out above the firing:

"STAND FIRM, DECEPTICONS! WE ARE FIGHTING FOR OUR RETURN TO CYBERTRON!"

Quickly the Decepticons rallied. They took cover among the machinery. The Autobots on the other hand were exposed in an empty section of the tunnel under the glare of the lights.

Optimus Prime acted swiftly. "The lights!" he cried. "Shoot out the lights!"

A blast of Autobot fire shattered the lights. Under cover of the darkness, they now found the Decepticons easy targets against the purple glow from the test equipment. But as soon as the Autobots tried to get close, they were driven back each time.

Optimus Prime called up Jazz on the radio. "Create a diversion!" he ordered.

"Wilco!" replied Jazz. "I'll draw them off with my photon rifle."

Then Spike's voice sounded in the radio. "Can you hold their attention just a little longer? I have an idea. When you get the word...get out of the tunnel FAST!"

"What's the plan?" said Jazz.

"The wagons!" said Spike. "Get me back to the quarry as fast as you can!"

Mystified, Jazz transformed, and as he bumped his way back up the old railway track, Spike explained. Jazz skidded to a halt, and Spike leapt out. He ran to the first of the wagons, jumped up, and heaved on the rusted brake wheel. He did the same on the others as Jazz transformed back to his robot shape. Jazz watched as a panting Spike pushed against the buffer of the last wagon. "You've done your bit, Spike," he said. "Allow me." And with one mighty thrust of his metal muscles he sent the whole train of wagons rumbling along the track, out of the quarry, and down the long slope to the tunnel.

As the wagons sped faster and faster, Jazz
signalled, "Jazz to Autobots! Now! GET OUT
FAST!"

The trucks rumbled across the road, lurched
round the last bend, and with a roar burst into
the tunnel. Decepticons were scattered in all
directions. The steel hoppers ploughed through
the ion-drive test rig, and the whole complex
exploded in a blinding glare of released energy. In
a cloud of dust the tunnel collapsed on top of the
wreckage.

Spike and Jazz joined the other Autobots. "Do
you think that this is the end of the
Decepticons?" asked Spike. "I'd like to think so,"
said Optimus Prime, "but I think we'll just have to
wait and see!"

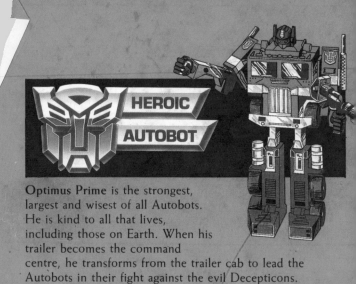

## HEROIC AUTOBOT

**Optimus Prime** is the strongest,
largest and wisest of all Autobots.
He is kind to all that lives,
including those on Earth. When his
trailer becomes the command
centre, he transforms from the trailer cab to lead the
Autobots in their fight against the evil Decepticons.

**Hound** transforms from a four-wheel-drive vehicle to the
Autobot scout robot. He is brave and loyal to the Autobot
cause and likes the planet Earth. Secretly, Hound would like
to be human!

**Sideswipe** transforms from a racing car to a warrior robot.
He and his twin brother, Sunstreaker, make a powerful
team in the never-ending battle against the Decepticons.

**Huffer** transforms from a trailer cab to become the Autobot
construction engineer. Although he will mutter and
complain, he is a strong and reliable worker.

**Jazz** transforms from a racing car to the Autobot special
operations agent. He takes on the dangerous missions and is
clever and daring. He likes Earth and is always looking to
learn more about the planet and its people.

**Gears** transforms from an armoured carrier to work as a
transport and reconnaissance robot. Like Huffer, he likes to
be miserable and find fault in everything, but he has great
strength and endurance.